Teacher's Pet

Terrance Dicks

The Adventures of Goliath

Teacher's Pet

Terrance Dicks
Illustrated by Valerie Littlewood

First edition for the United States and
the Philippines published 1992 by
Barron's Educational Series, Inc.

First published 1990 by Piccadilly Press Ltd.,
London, England.

All inquiries should be addressed to:
Barron's Educational Series, Inc.
250 Wireless Boulevard
Hauppauge, New York 11788

International Standard Book No. 0-8120-4820-2

Library of Congress Catalog Card No. 91-32665

Library of Congress Cataloging-in-Publication Data

Dicks, Terrance.
Teacher's pet / Terrance Dicks ; illustrated by Valerie Littlewood. — 1st ed. for the U.S. and the Philippines.
p. cm. — (The adventures of Goliath)
"First published 1990 by Piccadilly Press Ltd., London, England" — T.p. verso.
Summary: David's clumsy and lovable dog Goliath helps him get out of trouble with a seemingly mean math teacher and saves the teacher's job at the same time.
ISBN 0-8120-4820-2
[1. Dogs—Fiction. 2. Teachers—Fiction. 3. Schools—Fiction.] I. Littlewood, Valerie, ill. II. Title. III. Series: Dicks, Terrance. Adventures of Goliath.
PZ7.D5627Te 1992
[Fic]—dc20 91-32665
CIP
AC

PRINTED IN THE UNITED STATES OF AMERICA
2345 9770 98765432

CONTENTS

Chapter One

David Meets a Monster

David gave Goliath a farewell hug at the front gate. "Goodbye, Goliath, I'll see you after school. And be good! No following me."

Goliath's tail drooped sadly between his legs. He hated it when summer vacation ended and David went back to school. Heaving a massive doggy sigh, Goliath trotted back inside the house. It was nearly time for the cartoons on television.

David wasn't too happy himself as he trudged along the all-too-familiar route

to school. It was the beginning of a new school year, which meant new teachers.

Usually, it didn't make all that much difference. Some teachers were better and some were worse, and it all sort of evened out.

But this year was going to be different. David would have Mr. Paine for math—his very worst subject, and the most terrifying teacher in the entire school.

Mr. Paine was more than just another teacher. Mr. Paine was a monster—a legend.

For generations older kids had been saying to younger kids, "You wait till old Painey gets his hands on you!"

Math was the first class after recess and in the playground everyone in David's class was discussing the coming ordeal.

"He can't be *that* bad," said David's friend William uneasily. "They say he never shouts at you—and he hardly ever punishes anyone."

"You know why, don't you?" said David's other friend, Tom. "In old Painey's class, *no one ever dares to do anything wrong!* "

David didn't say anything. The end-of-recess bell rang, and the class went inside to meet their fate.

They sat waiting quietly in the classroom and suddenly Mr. Paine arrived. He didn't seem to enter in the normal way. He was just *there*, glaring at them.

He was amazingly tall and thin with spiky gray hair, piercing gray eyes, and a long pointy nose with glasses perched on the end. He looked like a fierce cockatoo David had once seen in the local pet shop. David had a sudden vision of Mr. Paine crouched up on a perch screeching, "Hello! Hello!"

He couldn't resist smiling at the thought, and right away Mr. Paine showed his amazing powers. "Something amusing you, David? Have you seen something funny? *Me* for instance?"

David gulped. "No, sir. Sorry, sir."

It was a bad start.

Mr. Paine swept the class with a laser beam glare. "I shall begin by taking you through a simple mathematical problem, step by step." It was something about two men called Bob and Jack filling a swimming pool with a couple of hoses. The pool was of such and such a size, and the water came out at a certain speed...

As usual, David's mind wandered off. He thought about the last time he'd gone swimming in the public pool. David liked swimming, but he didn't like swimming pools. He hated that weird chemical smell they all seemed to have. Now the ocean, that was different.

He thought about the first time they'd taken Goliath to the beach. They'd had a terrible job getting him to go in the water. Goliath was very timid for all his size, and he was firmly convinced that the waves were monsters trying to attack him.

Mr. Paine's voice interrupted his daydream. "And the answer, therefore, is..." He wrote the solution on the blackboard.

"Is that quite clear?"

Nobody said it wasn't. Nobody dared.

"Very well," said Mr. Paine. "So, if we make the swimming pool half as big again and take away one of the hoses, how long will it then take to fill the swimming pool?"

David couldn't help feeling sorry for Bob and Jack. They'd worked so hard filling that pool and now they had to do an even bigger one, and with only one hose. He wondered if they'd go for a swim when they'd finished.

"Time's up!" snapped Mr. Paine. He looked around the class, and somehow David just knew where that laser beam gaze would end up. "David, your answer please."

David looked at the exercise book in front of him. The page was completely blank.

"Well, David?" said Mr. Paine.

Chapter Two

A Bulldog Called Winston

The silence seemed to go on forever. Then David mumbled, "Sorry, sir, haven't finished."

Mr. Paine swooped down from the front of the class like a great bird of prey. He looked over David's shoulder at the blank page. Then he looked at David and shook his head in disbelief. "My stars!" he muttered. "My goodness!"

He went back to the front of the class. "Is it too much to hope for that someone has actually finished this exercise?"

One or two hands went up. Mr. Paine pointed. "Yes!"

The boy read out his answer. "Correct!" said Mr. Paine.

The lesson went on, but David didn't take much in. Luckily Mr. Paine didn't point to him again. David felt dazed. He'd made an utter fool of himself in the very first lesson, and now Mr. Paine would write him off as hopeless.

The lesson ended at last and the class filed out. As David passed his desk, Mr. Paine said, "David, stay behind please."

David hung back as the rest moved past him.

Mr. Paine was gathering up his things. He looked down at David, not angrily, but more as if David was a difficult problem he was determined to solve.

"When I have a new class to deal with, David, I study their school records. You seem to be getting good results in every subject but math."

David hung his head and muttered, "I just can't do math, sir."

"No!" snapped Mr. Paine, so suddenly that David jumped. "You just *think* you cannot do math. In fact, you have *decided* that you can't do it. Well, David, *I* have decided that you can, and you will! We shall just have to see who's right, won't we?"

"Yes, we will," thought David stubbornly, though he didn't dare say it out loud.

Mr. Paine pointed a long, bony finger at the door, and David shot thankfully out of the classroom.

William and Tom were waiting in the hall.

"What happened?" asked William.

"Did he punish you?" asked Tom.

"He threatened me," said David.

Tom looked puzzled. "With what?"

"It's too horrible to think about," said David with a shudder. "He threatened to make me understand math!"

As they hurried to their next class, William said, "Don't forget you two. We have our soccer practice tonight."

The thought of soccer cheered David up. At least there was something he was good at.

* * *

The private soccer practice was William's idea. He and Tom and David were all crazy about soccer, and it would soon be time for the school teams to be selected. William was very interested in what he called "scientific play"—he'd even got a book about it. So once or twice a week, the three of them took a soccer ball into the nearby park, not just to kick around but for some serious training. They practiced passing, dribbling, ball control, and all the other skills that make up a good player. William was in charge, a referee's whistle around his neck. Goliath was always a bit of a problem on these occasions. He loved soccer and would rush around the field dribbling the ball between his front paws. The trouble was, he was sort of a selfish player, never letting go of the ball once it was in his possession. "It's no good," said William finally. "We can't have a real practice while that big hairy hound keeps hogging the ball. He'll have to be the cheering section."

Goliath didn't think much of this idea at first, but by now he realized that if he sat on the sidelines for the actual practice, he'd be allowed to join in at the end. They had a good practice that day, and the horrors of the math class faded from David's mind. At the end of the session

they were practicing penalty kicks, and it was David's turn.

He booted the ball at the goal, high and hard—a little too hard, unfortunately. It missed the goal completely and whizzed across the path that ran alongside the field—just as a tall old gentleman in a straw hat passed by, walking his dog. The ball just clipped the edge of the straw hat, sending it spinning from the man's head. A freak gust of wind caught the hat and it floated away.

"Oh, no!" gasped David, and he hurried over to apologize, Goliath trotting behind him.

David picked up the straw hat, dusted it off and ran back to hand it to its owner. "Sorry about that—" He broke off in horror. The owner of the hat was Mr. Paine. He was also the owner of the old bulldog that sat wheezing on the grass nearby.

Goliath was trying to persuade the bulldog to play, by making little dashes at him, then running around him in circles. The bulldog didn't seem to be very impressed. In fact, he was ignoring Goliath altogether.

"Thank you," said Mr. Paine acidly, taking the now rather battered hat. "If you'll call off your animal, Winston and I will be on our way."

"It's all right, sir," said David hurriedly.

"Goliath's only playing. He won't hurt him. Here, Goliath!"

Ignoring him, Goliath made another dash at Winston. Suddenly, the old bulldog bared his teeth and gave one tremendous "Woof!" Goliath skidded to a halt, spun around, and dashed back to the safety of the soccer field.

"Winston may be getting old," said Mr. Paine, "but he can still look after himself. Heel, Winston."

Mr. Paine and his dog went on their way, and David followed Goliath back to the others.

"What was all that about?" asked Tom. "Who was the old guy with the bulldog?"

"That old guy was Mr. Paine."

William shook his head in mock despair. "I don't know, David. First you don't answer his problems, then you knock his hat off and Goliath chases his dog!"

"Just you wait till the next math class," said Tom cheerfully. "He'll really have it in for you now!"

"Thanks a lot," said David bitterly. "You're really cheering me up. I just can't wait."

Chapter Three

The Showdown

From then on, math class was sheer torture for David. Mr. Paine never seemed to leave him alone. The bony finger would point, the sharp voice snap, "David, your answer, please!"

David would struggle to come up with an answer, usually the wrong one. Mr. Paine would sigh wearily, and pass on to someone else—but he always came back to David before too long.

Soon David came to feel that his friends were right, and that Mr. Paine really did have it in for him. He thought of asking for a change of teacher, or even a change of school, but somehow he managed to struggle on.

Mr. Paine was very enthusiastic about what he called "the basics" and from time to time he had them chanting multiplication tables. Later in the lesson, he would suddenly point to someone at random and snap something like, "Nine nines?"

After a few sessions, even David found himself saying, "Eighty-one!" or whatever the answer was, *without even thinking about it*. Maybe Mr. Paine was trying to turn him into a human computer!

Things came to a head one Friday afternoon. Math was the last class that day, and for some reason Mr. Paine had changed his routine. He wrote just one amazingly complicated problem on the board. "As soon as you have produced the correct solution, you may leave," he announced. With just one problem between them and weekend freedom, the class set to work.

Jenkins, the class genius, finished the problem in ten minutes, had his answer checked, and quietly disappeared, giving the rest of the class a lofty wave and a superior grin.

One by one, the rest of the class followed him. As the lesson grew near the end, there was only one boy left in the classroom—David. He was still nowhere near finishing when the bell rang for the end of school. Thankfully, David stood up.

Mr. Paine didn't move. "Have you finished, David?"

"Well, no sir, but—"

"Then please sit down."

"Sir, you don't understand," said David desperately. "It's the soccer tryouts tonight. I've been practicing for weeks and if I'm late they won't let me try out."

"You may leave when you show me a correct solution to the problem—and not before..."

David sank back into his seat. All that work, all that practice, and now he wouldn't even get a chance to try out.

It just wasn't fair. Wildly he thought of defying Mr. Paine and dashing out anyway. But it was no use, he thought. Mr. Paine would tell Mr. Morrison the coach, another stickler for discipline. There was just no answer.

Suddenly David realized there was an answer—to solve the problem. If he could get it right in the next ten minutes, he could still be in time for the tryouts. But that was impossible, wasn't it? He couldn't do math.

David glared furiously at the problem—and something happened inside his head. It was like ice melting, or a log-jam breaking up. Maybe it was all the math Mr. Paine had been pounding into him, sinking in at last. Whatever the reason, the problem on the board stopped being frightening and mysterious and became—just a problem. Something you solved. You started at the beginning and worked your way through step by step.

David turned over a new page and began to write.

Fifteen minutes later he got up and put the exercise book down in front of Mr. Paine.

Mr. Paine checked quickly through the work, and drew a large red check mark beside the answer.

David shot out of the classroom, dashed to the locker room, got changed in a flash and ran out onto the field.

He was too late. Tryouts had already begun.

The track-suited figure of the coach bustled up. "There you are, David. You're in that group over there."

"You mean I'm not too late?"

"No, of course not. You've been doing something for Mr. Paine, haven't you? He warned me earlier you might be delayed."

David had never played better in his life. Somehow the confidence he'd gained by solving the problem carried over into his soccer and he seemed to be able to put the ball exactly where he wanted. When the tryouts were over, Mr. Morrison came up and said, "Well done, David. Your game's really improved. I think we'll find a place for you all right." Tom and William had made the team also.

"All thanks to my coaching," said William. "I thought you were done for David, when he gave us that problem."

"So did I," said David. "Still, you never know what you can do till you try!"

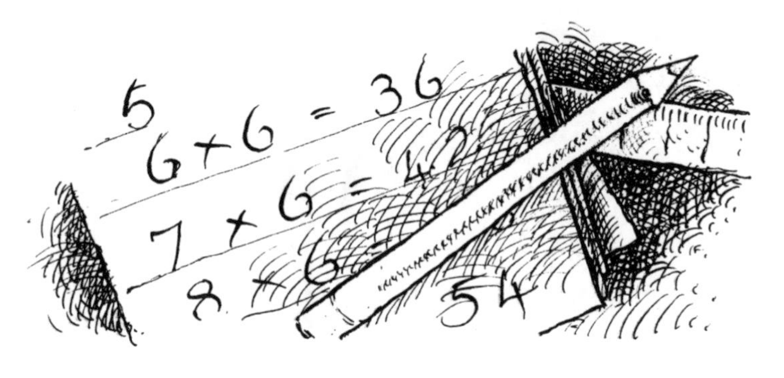

Chapter Four

Trouble in Class

All at once, things were going well for David.

Not only had he made the team, but Mr. Paine's lessons weren't torture anymore. He seemed to have stopped picking on David, calling on him no more and no less than anyone else. David, for his part, found he'd lost his blind terror of math. Now it was just a subject like any other.

Near the end of the term there was a big math test. The next day, Mr. Paine kept David back after class again. "I've just finished marking the test, David. I thought you might like an advance look at the results." He handed David a typed list.

David gave him a worried look. Were his results so awful he had to be told in private?

David studied the list, looking for his name, starting, naturally enough, at the bottom.

But he wasn't at the bottom of the list. He wasn't in the bottom half. He was actually in the top third.

He stood staring unbelievingly at the list.

Gently Mr. Paine took it back. "Your work has improved a great deal this year, David. Carry on like this and you should have nothing to worry about."

Then, in the next class, disaster struck—not so much for David, as for Mr. Paine.

Disaster arrived in the shape of Mr. Daniels, the Assistant Principal, a small, fierce red-headed man, known in the school as Discipline Dan. At the moment he happened to be Acting Principal. The real principal had slipped on a worn edge of the school steps and broken his ankle very badly. While he was away, Discipline Dan was in charge.

He was deadly serious about things like efficiency, economy, and, of course, discipline. He quickly proceeded to make everyone's life miserable. He started enforcing all the old rules about what you could and couldn't wear to school, and people got sent home for wearing jeans or running shoes.

He interfered with other teachers' classes, telling some they were too strict, others too easy. He even ran a campaign for extra homework.

Just before the end of the term,

Discipline Dan came into the classroom during one of Mr. Paine's "times table" sessions. He stared in amazement at the sight of rows of kids chanting, "One seven's seven, two sevens are fourteen, three sevens are twenty-one..." When they'd finished, Discipline Dan said, "Good heavens, I thought that kind of thing had died out ages ago."

"A lot of things have died out over the

years," said Mr. Paine. "Change isn't always for the better." He pointed at David. "Eight sevens?"

Luckily the computer worked perfectly and David snapped back, "Fifty-six!" without a second's pause.

Discipline Dan sniffed, but said nothing.

Mr. Paine worked them all extra hard for the rest of the lesson, while Mr. Daniels sat in the corner, getting on everyone's nerves. When the lesson was over he stayed behind for a word with Mr. Paine—and soon the departing class heard raised voices echoing down the hall. Naturally they all hung around listening.

Discipline Dan was yelling something about "Out-of-date teaching methods" and "Ineffective discipline" while Mr. Paine counterattacked with "Modernistic mumbo jumbo" and "Puffed-up little pipsqueak!"

Everyone scattered as the classroom door was flung open. Mr. Paine marched out and stalked off down the hall, followed shortly afterward by a red-faced Discipline Dan.

Despite all this fuss, the next day's math class, the last before the end of term, went on as usual. Then, at the end, Mr. Paine dropped his bombshell. "I wish to thank you—well, most of you—for all your hard work, and say goodbye. I have decided to take early retirement and will not be returning to school next term."

He looked at their amazed faces for a moment, then gathered his papers and marched out.

Chapter Five

David's Demonstration

As soon as school was over, David rushed home, had a hurried snack, and then took Goliath to the park. He wasn't just going for a walk though this time. He was looking for Mr. Paine.

He found the old teacher sitting on a bench by the children's playground, staring into space. Not far away, Winston was flopped on the grass, panting as usual.

David went and sat on the bench. Mr. Paine looked rather blankly at him. "Hello, David."

"I'm sorry to bother you out of school, sir, but I wanted to speak to you."

"Speak boy!" said Mr. Paine.

Goliath thought he meant him, and gave one of his loud barks. "Not you, Goliath," said David, and Goliath looked hurt. Drawing a deep breath, David went on, "You shouldn't pay any attention to old Discipline Dan, sir. They say the principal will be back soon and then things will go back to normal. He's nearly better now, you know. He's going to come to Open School Day tomorrow."

In front of them Goliath was running in dizzy circles around the patient Winston.

Mr. Paine didn't reply, and David went on, "That *is* why you're leaving, isn't it? We couldn't help overhearing..."

Mr. Paine cleared his throat.

"Mr. Daniels and I did have a rather heated exchange of views—but that was just the last straw. I've been feeling out of step with things for quite a while now."

"But you can't just go," protested David. "The school won't be the same without you."

"Nonsense," said Mr. Paine. "You were

there when I broke the news to the class. Hardly stricken with grief, were they?"

"They were just stunned, that's all."

Mr. Paine shook his head. "I'm not a popular teacher, David, I never have been. No one will miss me."

David looked at him in surprise. He'd never thought about Mr. Paine being popular or unpopular. He seemed above such things. He was just *there*—like Mount Everest. "It's not like that, sir," he said. "The thing is, no one knows anything about you. They don't even know about Winston."

"They think I'm just a sort of mathematical machine, do they?" said Mr. Paine grimly. "Well, let them! No doubt Mr. Daniels is right. The machine is out of date and should be replaced."

Tiring of their game, Winston chased Goliath away with a deep "Woof!" and flopped at his master's feet. Mr. Paine ruffled the old dog's head. "Besides, there's another problem. My landlady looks after Winston while I'm at school, and she has to go into the hospital for a minor operation. It's nothing serious, but she'll be away for quite a while and there'll be no one to look after Winston when school starts again. It's best if I go now."

Mr. Paine wouldn't discuss the matter anymore and soon it was time for David to go home. As he left he said, "I'll see you tomorrow, sir, for Open School Day."

The last day of school was the traditional Open School Day, a chance for parents and others to visit the school and enjoy various displays and exhibitions.

Mr. Paine sighed. "I'm not sure if I will be there."

"Please come, sir. Our class is leading the opening parade, remember? You mustn't miss that."

That night in bed, David talked the problem over with Goliath, who lay stretched out on his special mattress beside David's bed. Sometimes Goliath decided to sleep on the bed, and David ended up on the mattress. For all his size, Goliath was rather a timid dog, and he could never get to sleep unless David was nearby to look after him.

David often discussed his problems with Goliath, if only because it helped him to get things sorted out in his mind. He explained the situation about Mr. Paine and Goliath listened carefully, his head cocked to one side.

"He's going partly because of Winston, but mostly he thinks no one cares about him anyway," concluded David. "If only we could convince him he was wrong...

What can we do, Goliath?"

Goliath barked, the special deep ringing kind of bark he gave when David said, "Speak!"

David looked at him in surprise. "Speak? Tell him, you mean? I have but he won't listen."

Goliath barked again, louder this time.

"Speak louder?" said David. "Speak so loud he's got to listen, you mean?"

Goliath gave a third bark, even louder than the first two.

David's father's voice came floating up the stairs. "Can't you keep that hound quiet? He's drowning out the late night movie!"

David leaned out of bed and gave Goliath a hug. "Never mind, Goliath, you've given me an idea. Tomorrow we will 'speak'—so loud, everyone will have to listen...And since it was all your idea, you can come too!"

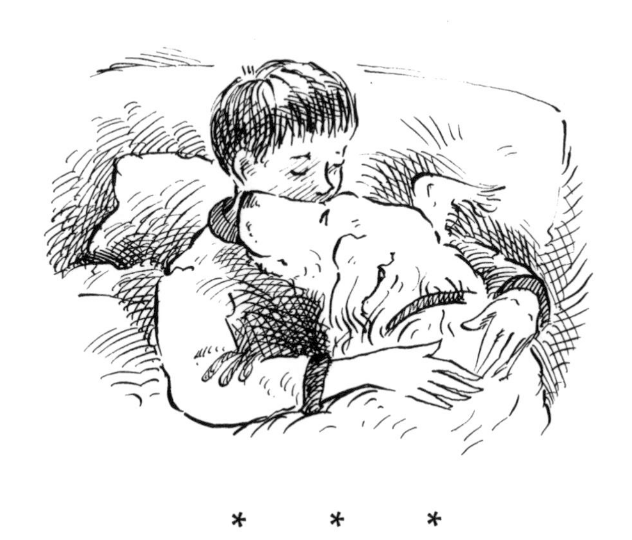

* * *

Open School Day didn't actually start till eleven o'clock, and everyone spent the first hours of the morning making sure the various exhibitions and displays were ready.

David had to work fast, convincing his classmates that something had to be done. Some of them were a little doubtful at first. "We'll get killed if we kick up a fuss on Open School Day," said Smithers, a rather shy boy. "The Principal will be there, and all sorts of VIPs."

"Why should we risk getting in trouble for old Painey?" said Thumwood, who was almost as bad at math as David had been. "We'll be better off without him."

"Our math won't though," said David. "Look what he did for me."

"That's right," said William. "He may be strict, but he gets you through your exams! He'll even get *you* through, Thumwood."

David's friend Tom came to their support. "Old Painey's like a national monument. We can't just let him be pulled down without a fight!"

"Right," said David. "Now listen, here's my plan..."

They were ready just in time.

The Open School Day ceremonies began with the staff, the school, and various VIPs gathered in the auditorium.

David and his classmates formed a line

outside. David had Goliath on his leash, a big paper scroll stuck in his collar.

The parade, which included all the noisier members of the school orchestra, was supposed to march in, parade around the auditorium and march out again.

And that's just what they did—the first part anyway. But instead of marching them out, David brought them to a halt before the platform.

At a signal from David, the members of his parade raised hastily-made banners, bearing such messages as "PRESERVE MR. PAINE!" and "PAINE MUST STAY!"

Then David led them in the special chant he'd just made up.

"Do we want old Paine to go?
No, no no! No, no, no!
Do we say that Paine must stay?
Yea, yea, yea! Yea, yea, yea!"

STAY STAY
STAY
STAY
PRESERVE
PAINE
DON'T GO
PAINE MUST STAY

Then he shouted, "Three cheers for Mr. Paine! Hip, hip, hooray! Hip, hip hooray! Hip, hip hooray!"

The whole school joined in.

Mr. Paine looked stunned. Discipline Dan looked furious, and the Principal looked baffled. He peered down from the platform. "What is all this fuss about?"

"It's about Mr. Paine," said David quickly. "He's leaving, only we don't want him to go and we don't think he really wants to either, so this is to tell him we want him to stay!"

"Mr. Paine leaving?" said the Principal.

A rumble of protest went up from the VIPs. "Mr. Paine can't leave!" growled one of the school board members. "I thought two and two made twenty-two when I joined his class, and I'm a certified public accountant now!"

"Of course Mr. Paine isn't leaving," said the Principal impatiently. "It's the first

I've heard of it. It's utter nonsense—isn't it, Mr. Daniels?"

"I'm afraid not," muttered Discipline Dan. "I didn't want to trouble you until you were back for good. We had a difference of opinion and Mr. Paine offered his resignation."

"And you accepted? You let Mr. Paine resign? *Mr. Paine*?" The principal drew a deep breath. "Mr. Daniels, there are people we can do without and people we can't do without and it's time you learned which was which! As for Mr. Paine leaving, there's no question of it! I refuse to accept his resignation. Now, can we get on?"

"There's just one more thing," said David hurriedly. He took the big scroll from Goliath's collar and handed it to Mr. Paine. "It's a petition, asking you not to go—signed by the whole class—and in fact, by the whole school!"

For once Mr. Paine was speechless.

The drum banged, the trumpets blared, Goliath barked, and David led his victorious parade out of the hall.

Chapter Six

Surprise Visitor

"Well, since everyone's making such a fuss I suppose I'll *have* to come back," said Mr. Paine. Despite his grumpy tone, David could tell he was really pleased. They were sitting on the bench by the playground, watching Winston and Goliath play.

"At least, I'd like to come back," Mr. Paine went on. "But my landlady won't be home for another week and I can't find anyone else to look after Winston."

David watched the two dogs romping

about—or rather, Goliath was romping. Winston, as usual, just sat there, wheezing.

David's mind went back to the time he'd gone to summer school. "Don't worry sir," he said. "I've got an idea..."

* * *

The whole class gave a cheer when Mr. Paine arrived for the first lesson of the new term. But the cheer turned into gasps of amazement when they saw who was with him.

Winston padded into the room and sat panting in front of the class.

Mr. Paine held up his hand and there was instant silence.

"This is my friend, Winston. The principal has kindly given permission for him to join us for this week—provided you don't let him distract you from your work too much. Now, just to prove to you that math isn't difficult—Winston, twenty-seven divided by nine!"

Winston barked—one, two, three times, and the class cheered again! David grinned. Like Winston, he'd been watching Mr. Paine's fingers, tapping against his leg. Winston was trained to give a bark for each tap.

Mr. Paine sent Winston to lie down in the corner. "There you are, then. If Winston can do arithmetic, you can too." He started writing a problem on the board.

At recess time Mr. Paine took Winston out into the playground, and everyone crowded around to see the dog who could do arithmetic. No doubt about Mr. Paine's popularity now, thought David.

Suddenly he heard a familiar bark, and a huge hairy shape hurtled over the school wall. Goliath landed in the playground with a thump, trotted over

to David, put his paws on his shoulders and licked his ear. "Oh no!" said David.

Mr. Paine came over. "What's going on?"

David pointed to Goliath, who was already running circles around Winston, watched by a crowd of delighted kids. "It's Goliath."

Mr. Paine blinked. "So I see. What on Earth is he doing here?"

"I think he suspected he was being left out of something," said David. "Anyway, I'm in trouble now! Goliath's seen that Winston's allowed in school. So, how will I ever convince him that he can't come too?"

About the Author

After studying at Cambridge, Terrance Dicks became an advertising copywriter, then a radio and television scriptwriter and script editor. His career as an author began with the *Dr. Who* series and he has now written a variety of other books on subjects ranging from horror to detection. Barron's publishes several of his series, including *The Adventures of Goliath, T.R. Bear, A Cat Called Max,* and *The MacMagics.*

More Fun, Mystery, And Adventure With Goliath–

Goliath's Birthday*
Goliath's fifth birthday is here. My, how dog years fly! A party is planned but will it go off without a hitch or will Goliath be his mischievous self? (Paperback only, ISBN: 4821-0)

Teacher's Pet*
David helps save his teacher Mr. Paine with the kind of help that only Goliath can give! (Paperback only, ISBN: 4820-2)

Goliath And The Burglar
The first Goliath story tells how Goliath becomes a hero when he saves his new family from a nasty burglar! (Paperback, ISBN 3820-7—Library Binding, ISBN 5823-2)

Goliath And The Buried Treasure
When Goliath discovers how much fun it is to dig holes, both he and David get into trouble with the neighbors, until Goliath's skill at digging transforms him into the most unlikely hero in town! (Paperback, ISBN 3819-3—Library Binding, ISBN 5822-4)

Goliath On Vacation
David persuades his parents to bring Goliath with them on vacation—but the big hound quickly disrupts life at the hotel. (Paperback, ISBN 3821-5—Library Binding, ISBN 5824-0)

Goliath At The Dog Show
Goliath helps David solve the mystery at the dog show—then gets a special prize for his effort! (Paperback, ISBN 3818-5—Library Binding, ISBN 5821-6)

Goliath's Christmas
Goliath plays a big part in rescuing a snow-storm victim. Then he and David join friends for the best Christmas party ever. (Paperback, ISBN 3878-9—Library Binding, ISBN 5843-7)

Goliath's Easter Parade
With important help from Goliath, David finds a way to save the neighborhood playground by raising funds at the Easter Parade. (Paperback, ISBN 3957-2—Library Binding, ISBN 5877-1)

Goliath And The Cub Scouts
Mystery abounds when David and his big, loveable dog Goliath attend a Cub Scouts meeting in a gym where a mysterious burglary takes place. Can Goliath help David solve the mystery? (Paperback only, ISBN 4493-2)

Written by Terrance Dicks and illustrated by Valerie Littlewood. Goliath books are in bookstores, or order direct from Barron's. Paperbacks $2.95 each, Library Bindings $7.95 each. (If marked with an * then price is $3.50. No Canadian Rights.) When ordering direct from Barron's, please indicate ISBN number and add 10% postage and handling (Minimum $1.75, Can. $2.00). N.Y. residents add sales tax. ISBN PREFIX: 0-8120

250 Wireless Boulevard, Hauppauge, NY 11788
Call toll free: 1-800-645-3476